D0183406

The Secret of Me

Amy Sparkes

Sandra de la Prada

9112000453970

For Coryn - wishing you many marvellous adventures!

5% of author royalties is being donated to Ickle Pickles Children's Charity

www.icklepickles.org
Reg. charity number: 1129763

A STUDIO PRESS BOOK

First published in the UK in 2021 by Studio Press Books,
an imprint of Bonnier Books UK,
The Plaza, 535 King's Road, London SW10 0SZ
Owned by Bonnier Books,
Sveavägen 56, Stockholm, Sweden

www.studiopressbooks.co.uk
www.bonnierbooks.co.uk

Text © Amy Sparkes 2021
Artwork © Sandra de la Prada 2021

1 3 5 7 9 10 8 6 4 2

All rights reserved
ISBN 978-1-78741-730-4

A CIP catalogue for this book is available from the British Library
Printed and bound in China

The Secret of Me

Amy Sparkes

Sandra de la Prada

STUDIO
PRESS

I have a question,
a question for me:
when I am BIGGER,
what will I be?

Maybe a **pirate** exploring the seas, finding new islands of coconut trees.

Perhaps I'll tame **dragons** and soar through the **sky**, past snow-dusted mountains and deserts so dry.

Or maybe I'll have
some adventures afar,
play with the planets
and cartwheel through stars.

I'll fly a balloon
and I'll win the first place
in the world's most amazing
hot air balloon race!

Perhaps I'll dream stories
of **unicorns** fair,
and paint **cheeky goblins**
with bright purple hair.

I could climb mountains.
Because I am BRAVE,
I'll find hidden secrets
inside a dark cave.

Or maybe build towers
that tickle the sky
and make homes for giants
who eat apple pie.

When I am BIGGER,
I know what I'll be.

Anything, anyone...

... as long as I'm me!